Dear Parents:

Congratulations! Your child is taking
the first steps on an exciting journey.
The destination? Independent reading!

STEP INTO READING® will help your child get there. The program offers
five steps to reading success. Each step includes fun stories and colorful
art or photographs. In addition to original fiction and books with favorite
characters, there are Step into Reading Non-Fiction Readers, Phonics Readers
and Boxed Sets, Sticker Readers, and Comic Readers—a complete literacy
program with something to interest every child.

Learning to Read, Step by Step!

Ready to Read   Preschool–Kindergarten
• big type and easy words • rhyme and rhythm • picture clues
For children who know the alphabet and are eager to
begin reading.

Reading with Help   Preschool–Grade 1
• basic vocabulary • short sentences • simple stories
For children who recognize familiar words and sound out
new words with help.

Reading on Your Own   Grades 1–3
• engaging characters • easy-to-follow plots • popular topics
For children who are ready to read on their own.

Reading Paragraphs   Grades 2–3
• challenging vocabulary • short paragraphs • exciting stories
For newly independent readers who read simple sentences
with confidence.

Ready for Chapters   Grades 2–4
• chapters • longer paragraphs • full-color art
For children who want to take the plunge into chapter books
but still like colorful pictures.

STEP INTO READING® is designed to give every child a successful
reading experience. The grade levels are only guides; children will progress
through the steps at their own speed, developing confidence in their reading.

Remember, a lifetime love of reading starts with a single step!

Step into Reading, Random House, and the Random House colophon are registered trademarks of Penguin Random House LLC.

Visit us on the Web!
StepIntoReading.com
rhcbooks.com

Educators and librarians, for a variety of teaching tools, visit us at RHTeachersLibrarians.com

ISBN 978-0-7364-3957-2 (trade) — ISBN 978-0-7364-8271-4 (lib. bdg.)
ISBN 978-0-7364-3958-9 (ebook)

Printed in the United States of America   10 9 8 7 6 5 4 3 2 1

Moana and Pua

adapted by Melissa Lagonegro

based on an original story by Suzanne Francis

illustrated by the Disney Storybook Art Team

Random House 🏠 New York

Moana loves
the ocean.
She dances
in the waves.

Gramma Tala teaches her
all about the ocean.
They love to dance
in the waves together.

Chief Tui has a basket
of piglets.
He needs to bring them
to the farmer.

Moana wants to help.
They will travel
to the other side
of the island.

Chief Tui and Moana
sail with the piglets.
One piglet is not eating.
Moana is worried.

She wants
to help him.
First she must help
steer the boat.

They sail
around the island.
The other piglets
squeal and eat.

But the tiny piglet
is still not eating.
Now Moana is
really worried.

Moana and Chief Tui
reach land.
They jump
into the water.

They pull the boat
to shore.
The tiny piglet watches.

They bring the piglets
to the farmer.
He puts them in a pen.
The tiny piglet
still will not eat.

Moana picks up

the little piglet.

Moana fills a leaf
with coconut milk.
She pours the milk
into the piglet's mouth.
He finally eats!

Moana and the piglet
become friends.
She names him Pua.

Moana takes good care
of Pua.

The farmer is glad.

He lets Moana keep Pua.

Moana, Chief Tui, and Pua
go back to the boat.
Moana takes the sail.
She guides them home.

The family watches
Moana care for
her new friend.

Moana feeds Pua.

She keeps him warm.

Moana and Pua play fetch
with coconuts and shells.

They make new friends.

They pretend
to go fishing.
They fill their net
with coconuts.

Moana and Pua

love watching the sunset.

Most of all,

they love being friends!